HIM STANDING

RICHARD WAGAMESE

RAVEN BOOKS
an imprint of CALGARY PUBLIC LIBRARY
ORCA BOOK PUBLISHERS

Library and Archives Canada Cataloguing in Publication

Wagamese, Richard
Him standing / Richard Wagamese.
(Rapid reads)

Issued also in electronic formats.
ISBN 978-1-4598-0176-9

I. Title. II. Series: Rapid reads.
PS8595.A363H54 2013   C813'.54   C2012-907303-2

First published in the United States, 2013
Library of Congress Control Number: 2012920187

Summary: When a Native carver agrees to produce a spirit mask
for a mysterious stranger, he falls under the spell of a dangerous
sorcerer from the Dream World.

*Orca Book Publishers is dedicated to preserving the environment and has
printed this book on Forest Stewardship Council® certified paper.*

Orca Book Publishers gratefully acknowledges the support for
its publishing programs provided by the following agencies:
the Government of Canada through the Canada Book Fund and the
Canada Council for the Arts, and the Province of British Columbia
through the BC Arts Council and the Book Publishing Tax Credit.

Design by Teresa Bubela
Cover image: Thunderbird Mask by Ojibway carver Mathew Esquega,
courtesy of the Squamish Lil'wat Cultural Centre.

ORCA BOOK PUBLISHERS
PO Box 5626, Stn. B
Victoria, BC Canada
V8R 6S4

ORCA BOOK PUBLISHERS
PO Box 468
Custer, WA USA
98240-0468

www.orcabook.com
Printed and bound in Canada.

16 15 14 13 • 4 3 2 1

For Debra—The magic in my world.

CHAPTER ONE

I got a trick with a knife I learned to do pretty good. It's not what you think. Despite all the crap about gangbangers and the gangbanger lifestyle, I got no part of that. No, the trick I do with a blade is that I make people. I can look at a perfect stranger for, like, maybe a minute, then turn around and carve his likeness into a hunk of wood. A perfect likeness. I've done it for lots of people. It's like I see them there. In the wood. Like they were there all the time. Like they were just waiting for me and my blade to come along and create them. It's a good trick.

Now, I ain't what you'd call established in a major way or anything. But this talent, or whatever it is, got me a regular gig on the boardwalk. Thing is, I didn't even have to get a permit like the rest of the buskers and the charcoal sketchers. No, me, I lucked out. I chose the one guy out of a thousand, that summer day, who could help me. I sat him down and did him for free. I didn't know who he was at the time. Took me half an hour. Turned out the cat was with the city licensing department. When I finished, he said he was willing to give me the license in a straight swap for the carving. I'm no stooge. I took it. I been working the boardwalk ever since.

It's a pretty good nickel. Once your name gets out, people actually come looking for you. Lucas Smoke. Imagine that? Straight shootin', regular citizens calling my name. Seeking me out. Anyway, I started turning out, like, four of these a day for fifty bucks apiece.

That's a two-hundred-dollar day, and that's nothing to sniff at. Beats freakin' workin', if you know what I mean.

Don't get me wrong. I never had anything against sweatin' and grindin' for a dollar if that's what a guy's gotta do. But there had to be options. It was my grandfather who turned me on to it. He was a carver. Did all these spooky faces he called spirit masks. They were big with the tourists. And then big with the galleries and collectors. Pretty soon my grandfather was rollin' in the dough. He was the only Ojibway on our reserve that had a house with three stories. Great big cedar-log house with floor-to-ceiling windows, overlooking the lake.

Then he handed me a knife one day and told me to make him in wood. I laughed. I was thirteen, and I had better things to do with knives. Like skinning a moose or filleting a fish. Something that had a purpose.

But he looked square at me the way grandfathers do and told me again to make him in wood. I don't know what happened. I know that I looked at him and I just saw him different. I saw angles and shadows and places where his face was irregular. I saw dips and planes and hollows. I started to carve. I had no idea what I was doing, but it was like my hands had a mind of their own. He said it was amazing. It was my grandfather who taught me everything I know about how to handle a blade. In fact, he gave me the knife. It's got a turtle-shell handle, and it's old. Really old. That's what he said. It was a traditional carver's knife. He said using it would connect me to the old-time magic of carvers. It's the knife I still use today.

That was seven years ago. My grandfather died when I was sixteen. Then the whole family started fighting over who got what. It made me sick. I missed the old man so much I ached all over. But all they could think about was the money, the house, the art and what it was worth. All I could think about was his hands. When he worked, they were a part of him but…not. That sounds crazy, but it was like they had their own spirit. They moved elegantly. That's a word he taught me. It means "energy set free." That's what he said. I could see that when he worked. And on a good day, I can see it in mine. Spirit moving in its own time.

So while the family squabbled, the whole thing ended up in court. And I booked it for the city. I didn't want any of my grandfather's things. I didn't want his money. I wanted him, and since I couldn't have him anymore, the reserve started to feel like some empty little backwater in the middle of nowhere. So I came to the city looking for any kind of job I could find. I was down to my last few bucks when I found the boardwalk.

Everywhere you looked, there were people doing weird and wonderful things. There were magicians, jugglers, a one-man band, contortionists and even a guy who drove nails into his head. They did it for the money and the applause. One day I sat on an empty bench and picked up a soft-looking piece of wood. I turned it over in my hands and started making a pretty woman in a hat who was looking out at the water a few yards away from me. Shavings were laid around my feet. There was a crowd gathered around me when I finished. The lady with the hat gave me thirty dollars. I did a couple more before the crowd drifted away. I came back to the rooming house where I live with almost a hundred bucks.

I met my girl on that boardwalk. Amy One Sky. She's a drop-dead gorgeous Ojib girl who works as a model and loves my work. She didn't even mind that I had next to nothing. She said I had a gift.

She said she knew people who could get me my own show in a gallery. So I started working on pieces. Amy even got a few sold for me, and it looked like I was on the fast road to being a real artist.

Then Gareth Knight showed up on the boardwalk, and everything got weird real fast.

CHAPTER TWO

It was one of those picture-postcard days. The sun was blazing, and the waves were roiling in, all foamy and white against the blue. A slight breeze. People everywhere. And the smell of hot dogs and candy floss. It was a circus atmosphere. Everyone got turned on by it. You could feel the energy all along the boardwalk. I did three pieces by two o'clock. There was a ring of hangers-on around me constantly. I dug that action. By this time Amy had put me in touch with people who knew people, and my carvings were becoming known. I had orders, for Pete's sake. But I still loved the feel of the boardwalk. It was wild and outrageous. There were rock bands that plugged in and played. It put people in the mood to spend. To throw money in the hat I laid at my feet. I felt at home there.

There was this fat old guy who must have been in his seventies. He had a face built of wrinkles on top of wrinkles on top of at least three chins. He sat in the chair in front of me and asked me to do him. All I could think was that I didn't have a big enough piece of wood. But it was a fabulous face. There was so much detail to work with. His eyes sat behind globs of flesh and shone with a dark light, and his ears were clumps of meat. Fabulous. I was so captivated by it that all I could do was look at him.

"This magnificent face asks the best of you," I heard a voice say. "You aren't thrown off by a challenge, are you?"

I looked up from studying the fat guy's face. A man dressed all in black and leaning on a cane was looking straight at me. He had on an old-style fedora, the brim curled down over one eyebrow. A tiny sprout of beard grew just under his lower lip. His eyes were dark and glimmered in the light.

"I say you can't do it," he said. "In fact, this here says you can't."

He held up a roll of bills, and the crowd gasped. He smiled.

"I like a challenge," I said. "Let's see what I can do."

I picked up my biggest piece of pine and set it in my lap. The fat man splayed his feet apart and got comfortable in the chair. The sun cut deep shadows between his wrinkles. It would be hard. I looked up, and the man in black grinned at me and waved the roll of bills. I set to work.

Sometimes, when the work is good, I go way beyond time and space. I go somewhere else. I don't know where that place is, but I definitely lose contact with Earth. I exist in a separate world. A dream world, I guess, is the best way to describe it. Grandfather said that it is where stories are born. He said that when I carve, what I'm really doing is telling a story in wood. So the storytelling place is where I go when I'm really working well.

This time I was gone right away. I had no sense of time passing. I had no sense of concentration. I had no idea what people were doing around me. All I had was this fascination with my subject. The more I let myself feel that, the more I felt myself slip away and become one with it. Corny? It used to seem that way to me. But I came out of that storytelling place the first time and held a finished piece in my hand that blew me away. I don't think it's corny anymore.

I don't know how long I was gone. I do know that it felt like my hands were on fire when I put the knife down. My breathing was ragged and I felt dizzy. But the crowd applauded when I set the likeness down on the small folding table I kept at my side. The fat man beamed with pleasure, mopped his face with a hankie and handed me fifty dollars. The carving was spectacular. I had caught every detail perfectly. The wood seemed to flow with the energy of that face.

The man in black nodded. He seemed pleased too. When he stepped forward and held out the roll of bills, the crowd around us clapped again. I stood up, took the money and reached out to shake the man's hand. It was cool, dry and taut with strength. He dipped his head and raised one hand to the brim of his hat in salute. A very gentlemanly move.

"An honor to watch you work," he said. "Gareth Knight is my name."

"Lucas Smoke," I said. "Thanks for this."

I waved the roll of bills. The one on the outside was a hundred, and I wondered if they all were.

"I know who you are," he said. "I've been watching the growth of your craft."

"Always nice to meet a fan."

"Not a fan, Mr. Smoke. More like an employer. I have a commission for you."

"Really? What did you have in mind?"

"A spirit mask. Like your grandfather did."

"You knew my grandfather?"

He offered a small smile.

"His work reached a great number of us."

"Us?"

"A circle of like-minded associates."

"I don't get it."

"You will. If you accept my offer."

"What exactly is this offer?"

"Ten times what's in your hand. Examine it when you get home. Call the number on my card."

He handed me a shiny black card with only his name and a telephone number on it.

"I don't do spirit masks," I said.

He smiled, and I suddenly felt very cold.

"You will," he said. Then he turned and disappeared into the crowd.

CHAPTER THREE

There were fifteen hundred bucks in the roll. In hundreds and fifties. It was more money than I had ever seen in one place at one time. I held it in my hands and fanned it wide. I could feel an excitement I had never felt before start to glow in my belly. Amy watched me with a small smile on her face.

"You're like a little kid on Christmas," she said.

"Feels like it. I mean, ten times this will be more money than I've earned in my life," I said.

"Yes. But you have to earn it."

"What do you mean?"

"I mean you have to quit sniffing the advance and get to work, bucko."

We laughed. It felt good holding a wad of money and knowing there was more coming. All I had to do was get to work. But that bothered me. I still didn't know exactly what Gareth Knight wanted. I handed his card to Amy. She looked at it and rubbed her thumb across its slick surface.

"So this guy dressed all in black challenges you to carve a face. Then he hands you fifteen hundred bucks in a roll and offers you ten times that to do what your grandfather did?" she asked.

"Yeah, with a weird reference to a circle of like-minded associates."

"He sounds freaky," she said. "We should call him."

"Right now?"

"Why wait?" she asked. "I would never go on a shoot for someone I didn't know. Not unless I got full particulars."

"I suppose. Sure. Why not? Get the ball rolling here." I picked up the card and punched the numbers into the phone and held it to my ear.

Then a funny thing happened. We both heard the ring of the phone at the other end of the line. It rang just outside my door. At the same moment, there was a knock. I looked at Amy. She was as shocked as I was. I put the phone down and went to the door. I opened it to find Gareth Knight leaning on the jamb, waving his phone idly in his hand.

"You rang?" he asked and smiled.

"How did you know where I lived?" I asked.

He laughed. Then he straightened, adjusting his attire. He was still in black, but now he was dressed in jeans, boots, a T-shirt and a tuxedo jacket. A porkpie hat sat on his head at a rakish angle.

"I like to know where my money is going. I have associates who undertook to find that out for me. Nice accommodations, by the way. Very grungy in a struggling-artist sort of way. Nice aroma of cabbage, socks and grease."

He looked at Amy and bowed slightly.

"I'm a bit surprised to find you here, my dear."

"Well, I come with the territory," she said. "And besides, Mr. Knight, Lucas lives here because he wants to, not because he has to."

"I see. To soak up the atmosphere. Feed the muse, I suppose."

"Something like that," I said. The guy was starting to irritate me. "What are you doing here, anyway?"

"Same thing you were doing with the telephone, Lucas. Getting the ball rolling here."

Amy and I looked at each other in surprise. He had used the same words as me. He watched us with an amused expression.

"Now, may I come in to discuss details, or are you and Ms. One Sky going to keep me outside in this lovely hallway all day?"

"How do you know my name?" Amy asked. She sounded angry.

Knight touched the brim of his hat and nodded.

"Come now, Ms. One Sky. One needn't look far to find your face. And one needn't look far beyond that to find out who the face belongs to. A wonderful face, I might add. You should carve her, Lucas."

I stepped back to let him in. He strode by and inspected the room. It had never been much. Just a bed and a dresser, a small closet, an armchair and a table that held my carving tools and a few pieces of wood. He nodded, almost as if he liked it. Then he turned and regarded us with a raised eyebrow.

"Shall we discuss our arrangement?"

Amy and I sat on the bed, and Knight lowered himself slowly into the armchair. He looked at me calmly. I stared back at him for a long moment. Finally I cleared my throat.

"You're willing to pay me fifteen thousand for a spirit mask, even though you understand that I've never done a spirit mask. That's what it is, unless I missed something."

"Wonderfully summarized, Mr. Smoke."

"So what is it that you want exactly?"

"I want a legend brought to life."

"Excuse me?" I asked abruptly.

Knight grinned.

"I mean, I want the essence of a legend brought to life. As you do with all your work, Lucas. I want you to bring the spirit of a story forward."

"Which story is that?" I asked.

"That's where the work comes in, I'm afraid."

"Meaning?" Amy asked.

He looked at her and gave her a huge and dazzling smile. She blushed, and he smiled even harder.

"You have to dream," he said. "You have to allow yourself to inhabit the dream world. There you will find the legend and the story I want brought to life in wood. Your grandfather understood this way. It was the key to his work."

"He never shared that with me," I said.

"A pity. You'll have to learn it on your own then."

"How do I do that?"

"Sleep," he said, "perchance to dream."

"I've never dreamed very clearly," I said.

"You will."

"How can you be so sure?"

He leaned back in the chair and crossed one of his legs over the other. He made a steeple with his fingers and braced it under his chin.

"Because your grandfather left you his gift. It's rare, Lucas. Rare."

"Why should I believe that?"

"I can think of fifteen thousand reasons," he said and laughed.

CHAPTER FOUR

Neither Amy nor I were comfortable once Knight had left. He was a mystery. We knew nothing about him, except that he could throw around a lot of money. While that was okay with me, I didn't like feeling that I was on the outside of things. Dream? What was that supposed to mean? My whole gig was built on carving what I could see. If something was right in front of me, I had no trouble making it appear in wood. But this? This was just weird.

We spent the rest of the day trying to distract ourselves. Amy led me to our favorite secondhand shops, the thrift stores and flea markets where I bought all my clothes and stuff. Paying full price for things wasn't something I liked to do. Besides, things always felt better to me when I knew they had a life before I got them. I guess that's why I got so good at carving—I could feel history in things.

We ate at Amy's apartment. She's a good cook. She cut a steak into thin strips and stir-fried it with broccoli, snow peas, peppers, onions, mushrooms, tomatoes and spices that made it all tangy and hot. I loved it. Then we curled up on her couch and listened to music in the dark. That's one of the things we like the most. We turn off everything but the stereo and let the music flow over us in the darkness. It's really cool. You get right inside the music that way, and you hear things in it that you don't normally hear. We don't talk. We just listen. We spend hours that way.

After that I walked home.

Gareth Knight was still on my mind. I wanted to do the job. But there was something about it that bugged me. Knight never said anything straight. He just kind of laid something out there and expected you to run with it or let it hang. And talking about my grandfather—that bugged me a lot. The memory of my grandfather was so special that I never spoke of him. Even to Amy. All of us have things so precious we keep them to ourselves. Things we don't want to lose. Things we don't want changed from the way we remember them. I guess I didn't want anything to change about the way I remembered my grandfather. So I never spoke of him.

When I got home, I read for a while. I was actually afraid to sleep. I didn't think I bought the mumbo jumbo Knight had talked about. But it kept me awake. Legends brought to life? Legends were stories. Teaching stories. But they were just stories. There weren't real people in them. They were all dream people.

I tossed and turned once I shut the light off. I thought about getting up and working on something. Instead, I just lay there. Finally, after an hour or so, I drifted off.

I found myself on a riverbank in the moonlight. It was made of stones. There was a tall cliff behind me and a narrow path twisting its way upward. Across the river was another cliff, but this one was less steep. There was a thick carpet of trees on its face. The moon hung right over the middle of the water. The river had eased out of a long, sweeping turn, and the current was slow. It was summer, and the night was cool but not uncomfortable.

There was a canoe on the beach a few yards away from me. I suddenly wanted to paddle. I walked over and pushed the canoe into the water. I waded in knee-deep and stepped over the gunwale and into the canoe. I began to paddle. I could see the reflection of the moon on the calm water. A light breeze barely disturbed the peaceful night air.

But suddenly the wind rose. It came blustering out of the upstream sweep of the river and quickly turned the water to chop. The canoe begin to buck in the waves. The current grew stronger. The canoe was pushed downstream. Nothing I could do would change its course. The river churned and the canoe dipped crazily. I heard laughter. I looked around, but there was no one there. The laughter boomed out across the water.

Then I heard the thunder of a waterfall. I could see the spume rising in clouds a half mile ahead of me. The roar of it grew louder. There was nothing I could do to stop the canoe. The laughter rumbled off the cliffs all around me.

I flailed at the water with the paddle. The canoe hurtled forward. I felt my insides turn to water. Just as it reached the edge of the waterfall, I looked up. There was the face of a man in the moon. He was laughing. That's all I saw before the bow dropped and the canoe plummeted. I hit the pool at the foot of the falls and was pushed down deeper and deeper, as if by a giant hand. The frigid water produced a burning sensation.

I spun in the crazy current. I had no idea which way was up. Then I heard a voice say, "Open your eyes." That's all. It was a deep bass voice. Commanding. I opened my eyes. All I could see was eerie, dark blue. Then I saw the moon. I kicked hard toward it. As I got closer to the surface, the image became clearer. Then I saw the face. A shaman's face, painted black with three wavy red lines running down its right cheek. Looking down at me from the face of the moon.

"Do you see me?" the voice asked.

I clawed frantically for the surface. "Yes," I said.

"Bring me to life," it said.

"I can't," I said.

"Then die."

I felt icy hands push me deeper into the pool. My lungs wanted to explode. The moon had vanished. There was only the terrible dark of the water.

I woke up bathed in a cold sweat.

CHAPTER FIVE

At first, it was only dreams. They seemed to come even before I was fully asleep. All I had to do was close my eyes, and I was deep in the shimmer of light and color. Each of them was a story. Each of them had something to do with the shaman. I was in them as an observer. But I could see everything. I knew the man had power. I knew that he was a wizard, a sorcerer. I knew that he had lived a long time ago, before white people came to North America. I knew that he was cold. Heartless. I knew that he was mean.

But they were such grand dreams. I saw parts of the life my people had led many years ago. I saw trappers and hunters. I saw canoe makers, drum builders, toolmakers, hide tanners and men who were born to fight. Everywhere I looked in those dreams, I felt as though I was there. It was like they were shining a light on my own history, and I found myself eager to go to them, to find myself in them, to be among those people.

Those people included the man with the painted face. He carried a powerful magic. He lived alone, apart from the people, and when the smoke rose from his wigwam, the people seemed to creep around their camp. Songs and drumming and strange incantations came from that lodge then. Sometimes it would shake as though there was a violent struggle going on inside. The people averted their eyes. No one spoke. Everyone was afraid. But I couldn't take my eyes off that small wigwam in the trees.

Amy began to notice a change in me.

"You're so quiet lately," she said. "Is everything all right?"

"It's fine," I said. I was scraping a bevel-edged chisel along a line of wood and didn't look at her.

"It doesn't feel fine, Lucas. You feel far away from me."

"I'm busy," I said.

"You're always busy lately. But I never see anything get done. You stare off into space and rub the edge of a tool on wood, but you don't create anything."

I stood up suddenly. I could feel the raw, dark edge of anger in my gut.

"Are you going to start telling me how to work?" I asked. It didn't feel like my voice.

She sat back farther in her chair. She looked at me wide-eyed.

"You never raised your voice at me before," she said quietly.

I felt guilty. The anger had risen in me before I knew it was even there.

"I'm sorry," I said in my own voice. "This whole project has got me anxious, and I was never anxious about a piece before."

"It's the money, isn't it?"

"Yeah. That and Knight and the damn dreams."

"What dreams?"

I looked out the window at the skyline of the city. I spoke without looking at her. I told her about the vision of the camp and how it almost felt like I'd been transported back in time. How real the people and their lives seemed. I told her about the man with the painted face. I left out the part about the wigwam shaking and the feeling of blackness that fell over everything when that happened. I told her everything except the hold these dreams were starting to have on me. Like I needed them. Like I couldn't wait to get back to them.

"Knight told you to dream," she said. "He said you would."

"I haven't seen the legend though," I said.

"Maybe the legend is in the lives of the people."

"Too ordinary," I said. "Knight's after something heavy."

"Heavy as in what?" she asked.

I spun in my seat so fast, it shocked both of us. I stood up. Suddenly I felt heavier, bulkier, taut with muscle. My face felt like a chunk of stone. It was a heady feeling. I felt incredibly powerful. The voice that came out of me was harsh and sharp like a hiss.

"There are powers and secrets best not spoken, girl child."

Amy stood up and backed away from me. Her hand was at her throat, and her eyes were huge and scared-looking. I took a step toward her. She held the other hand out to keep me at arm's length.

"Don't," she said.

"Amy, I…I…" I stuttered.

"Just don't, Lucas. Don't do or say anything."

I felt smaller then, back to my usual size. My body sagged. There was a feeling in my head like the moment after an accident happens and you wonder where you are. I still had the chisel in my hand. I looked at it dumbly and laid it on the table. She was watching me closely. When I slumped into my chair, I saw her slowly start to relax.

"You called me girl child, Lucas. You never speak like that."

"Sorry," I mumbled.

"And your face? Your face was wild. Your eyes were almost red. I thought you were going to attack me with the chisel."

"I wouldn't," I said.

"*You* wouldn't, no."

"What's that supposed to mean?"

"I mean, I've never seen you react like that. It's like you were someone else. Someone I don't want to know."

I stared at the floor. I felt as though a chunk of time had been ripped from my life. It was as though I'd been pushed to the sidelines and forced to watch as things went on. As though I had no power to step off those sidelines and say or do anything different. But I couldn't tell her that. It made no sense to me. If it made no sense to me, it was sure not going to make any sense to her. I felt sure of that.

"I'm just stressed," I said. "I'll get some better sleep tonight and I'll be fine."

"This work isn't good for you. It scares me. You scare me."

All I could do was look at her and nod.

CHAPTER SIX

One morning my hands took on a life of their own. I'd found a nice piece of cedar that was large enough for a life-size mask. I split it with a tree-felling wedge and a small sledgehammer. I had to be careful. I wanted a perfect half round to work with. I needed the grain in the wood to be consistent and clear. I carefully chiseled the bark off. I moved slowly. I tapped the end of the chisel lightly, then guided it forward with my hands so the bark would come off easily. It took some time, but I ended up with a glistening, reddish surface with a fine grain. I'd never done this before. But somehow I knew how.

That didn't bother me. What bothered me was how I suddenly was able to just carve at will. Normally there was a subject, someone I could look at, that made the magic happen. But now there was nothing. There was only the recollection of the dreams. There was only the painted face. I tried to go through the specifics of the dreams. I wanted to figure out which legend Gareth Knight wanted me to carve. But all I could see was the dim painted face of the man in the wigwam. That's when my hands began to really move on their own.

I hadn't had a clear look at him since the first dream of the waterfall. Even that wasn't detailed enough. The face was flat. It had no edges or angles or hollows, and I didn't know what the bone structure was. All I saw was the leering, painted face. But my hands knew what to do. I sat there for hours every morning. It was like I fell into a spell. Time just disappeared. I don't know what happened to me during those times. But I do know that by the time I came out of them, there were shavings all around my feet. And I felt thick. Like my blood was sludge. Like my head was stuffed with cotton. Opening my eyes was like coming out of a coma. It was like I had left the world behind me. I felt odd, out of shape, not comfortable in my own body.

Every morning I would wake and sit with my coffee, looking out my window over the neighborhood. Every morning I would try to get a fix on the face. It wasn't a legend, but it was the one thing that kept coming to me. I couldn't shake it. I was worried Knight would call off the deal. I wanted that money. I wanted it bad.

Then I would move to my work table, and the day would disappear.

One day, after about a week of this, the telephone rang. I didn't answer it. I couldn't. Nothing existed for me but the mask, the face. I couldn't take my eyes from the work I was doing. It rang again. I let it ring. It rang three times before I could break out of the trance I was in to pick it up. Finally I picked it up.

"Yes?" The word came out of me dully.

"Is that you, Lucas?"

"Yes." It was the same thick voice.

"Lucas?" It was Amy. "Are you all right? You sound different."

"Yes," I said again. It seemed to be all I could say.

"Lucas, you're scaring me. I haven't seen you in nearly a week. You don't call. You don't answer voice messages, and you sound like you're stoned."

"Yes," I said.

"I'm coming over there right now."

I lay the phone in its cradle and stared at the wall.

I was still doing that when Amy walked into the apartment. I turned slowly to look at her. She shrank back against the door.

"Oh my god," she said. "Lucas."

"What?" I asked. I tried to smile, but the muscles in my face felt odd.

She walked toward me slowly. Her eyes were wide. "Your face," was all she said.

"What about my face?" My mind was clearing now that she was here.

"It's different."

"Different how?"

"It's older. It's definitely older."

"Can't be," I said, coming back to myself. "It's only been a few days."

She looked around the room. Except for the mess on my work table, the place looked tidy. When she came to sit across from me, there was a worried look in her eyes.

"You haven't been eating," she said. "There're no dirty dishes and your garbage is the same as the last time I saw it."

"No time," I said. "All I've been doing is working. Sleeping. Dreaming. Working."

"Dreaming about what, Lucas?"

"Don't know. Can't find the legend. Only got a face."

"What face?"

"The painted man. That's all I got. Painted man's face."

"Can you show me what you've done so far?"

I got up sluggishly. My body felt that same odd heaviness, and I couldn't get my feet to move. Finally I summoned enough strength to walk slowly over to the work table. The mask was covered with a black cloth. I didn't know where the cloth had come from. We stood side by side looking at it, and I could feel Amy's worry.

"That's it," I said. "The mask. The mask of the painted man's face."

"Is it finished?" Amy asked.

"No," I said. "It seems to be taking a really long time."

"Have you heard from Gareth Knight?"

"No. But he'll be pleased that I'm working."

"Even if it's going as hard and slow as you say?"

"Yes." I said it in the dreamy, detached voice she had heard on the phone.

She looked at me. Then she reached out and slowly pulled the black cloth from the carving. I heard her moan. I heard a sob in her throat. She looked at me with eyes brimming with tears.

"Lucas," she said shakily.

When I looked at the carving, I was staring at a blurred outline of my own face.

CHAPTER SEVEN

I sat there in disbelief. I'd worked so hard. It felt like the hardest work I had ever done. Now, there was just my face. I thought I was carving the painted man. I thought I was entering the dreams and coming out with a better idea of how to bring him to life in the wood. Amy and I sat there not knowing what to say. I felt beaten. I felt terrified. The week had been one long blur, and this was all I had to show for it. Amy looked scared. Plumb scared. She put both hands to her face and stared without blinking at the mask.

"I don't understand," she said quietly.

"Me neither," I said.

"I don't think you should do this anymore."

"I can't stop now."

"Why? It's not good for you, Lucas."

"There's too much on the line," I said.

"It's just money. You're a talented artist. You'll get more work. This is just weird, and it's not affecting you in a good way." She reached out and touched me lightly on the arm.

What happened next shocked both of us. I pushed her arm away with a sweeping motion and reached out and grabbed her by the shoulders. I stared hard into her eyes. The muscles in my face tightened so hard, I thought they would snap. I scowled. I shook her hard. There was a cold hardness in my chest. I was shaking. The voice that came out of me wasn't mine.

"The doorway is open. It will stay open, girl child. When I emerge, you will see real power!"

Amy scrambled out of my grip. She backed into the corner and stared wide-eyed at me. When I took a step, she held both hands out in front of her to ward me off. My feet were heavy, bulky. My arms and shoulders were tight. The scowl was still on my face. I put my hands up to my face and clutched both temples. I was terrified and sick and suddenly very weak. Before I knew what was happening, I had collapsed onto my knees in the middle of the room and was shaking violently.

"What's happening to me?" I howled.

"Not exactly feeling like yourself, Lucas?" I looked up. Gareth Knight stood in the doorway. We hadn't heard the door open. He was still dressed in black. The room felt colder all of a sudden. Amy strode over to kneel beside me. "The work is proceeding well, I see," Knight said.

Amy put her arms around me, and we watched as Knight stepped over to my work table. He laid a hand on his chin as he studied the mask. There was a small grin at the corners of his mouth, and he nodded.

"Very good," he said. "The spirit is growing stronger. Any interesting dreams lately, Lucas?"

"He's not going to do your work anymore," Amy said, standing up to face Knight. "You can keep your commission."

Knight smiled.

"Very bold, Ms. One Sky," he said. "I think I like that. But you see, Lucas and I have a gentleman's agreement. Don't we, Lucas?"

He tilted his head a little and looked at me. His eyes seemed to swim. They were like black seas. I felt I was being swept up in their tide.

"Yes," I said dully.

"You see, Ms. One Sky? He understands the nature of our deal. And besides, you really want to see this through, don't you, Lucas?"

"Yes," I said again. The word slid from my mouth with a hollow sound.

"Not a very wordy reply, but you can see he wants to do the job," Knight said. "It's not a good idea to cross an artist when he wants to create. It's not good to get between them and their work."

"He doesn't know what he's saying," Amy said. "Can't you see that?"

"Oh, I think Lucas knows exactly what he's saying. Don't you, Lucas?"

I looked at him. I stared into his eyes. Now they were glittering. I couldn't look away. I felt pulled deeper into them. My head felt cloudy, dreamy. I held his look and stood up slowly. When I did, I felt the odd heaviness in my body, and the room seemed suddenly smaller.

"The doorway is open," I said, and I heard Amy gasp.

Knight smiled again and broke the look.

"Yes. The doorway is open. You want to keep it open, don't you? And you won't let Ms. One Sky talk you out of it, will you?"

"The doorway will remain open. It will be finished. The girl child will not stop it." The voice was cold and stern. Amy stepped away from me.

"Who are you?" she asked Knight. "Where did you come from?"

"I'm just a simple art lover, my dear," Knight said. "As to where I came from, well, where do we all come from, Amy child? Are we not the same?"

"We're not the same," she said. "We don't walk around scaring people for the thrill of it. And I'm not a child."

"No. You're not. You're an adult. Just like Lucas is an adult. Free to make choices, free to decide what he wants and what is good for him."

"You've got him under some kind of spell or something," Amy said.

Knight laughed. It was a wild, rollicking laugh. But his eyes showed no humor. They were cold and flat and hard. He crossed one leg behind the other and leaned on the cane he carried.

"There is no spell. There is only desire. Your desire is to finish the mask, isn't it, Lucas?"

"Yes," I said dreamily.

He nodded. Amy looked at me and I felt my head clear. When we looked at the doorway, Knight had vanished.

CHAPTER EIGHT

"I'm so worried," Amy said.

Soon after Knight left, my head had begun to clear. I recalled everything that had happened, but I could make no sense of it. It felt as though I had only been an onlooker. Now, sitting at the table sipping tea with Amy, I was worried too.

"It's like I can't do or say anything when that guy's around," I said.

"We need to find a way to get you out of this," Amy said.

"I don't think there's a way. The guy scares me actually. I kinda think he's a half step away from crazy."

"I think he's already there. But I think what we need to do is get out of here for a while. You need groceries anyway. Let's do the market thing."

"Good idea," I said.

I was starting to feel back to myself, glad for her company and eager for some regular routine. Going to the market was one of our favorite things. We always rode our bikes. We got to pedal through our favorite parts of the city, and both of us enjoyed the trips. I was more than ready for an outing.

"Let's do it. We can get some of those muffins you like."

She smiled, but there was still a grave look in her eyes.

The day was brilliant with sunshine. There was only a hint of a breeze, and the sidewalks were filled with shoppers and people busy with their lives. It felt good to be out among them. We stuck to the bike lane and pedaled slowly, side by side. I took in the sights that I never seemed to grow tired of. When you're down to your last dime like I had once been, you get to like simple things. When your butt is on the sidewalk, even simple things seem a thousand miles away from you. Riding a bike and seeing so much activity was a pure pleasure.

The market was in one of those cool areas where there were bookstores, cafés, art shops, clothing boutiques and music stores. The people were mostly young, and there was a nice energy. No one ever looked twice at you, so you could just settle, feel relaxed and go about your business. That's why I liked going there. We found a rack to lock our bikes in and walked hand in hand to the market.

Amy had turned me on to really good food. I was just a regular Kraft Dinner and tuna kind of guy before I met her. A can of beans and wieners was a big night for me. But Amy knew about all these different sorts of veggies and fruits, crackers, cheeses, soups and things I never would have imagined in a million years. So shopping with her was like exploring. I never knew what we'd come out with.

We separated, and I took my time browsing the aisles. I liked the language of food. There were all kinds of cool words, like *wasabi*, *cannelloni* and *gourd*. I liked the way they felt on my tongue. One of my favorite things was to grab a can or a box and repeat the words on the label to myself. I was doing that when I saw a tiny lady down the aisle, trying to reach something on the top shelf. She couldn't get at it.

She looked to be about eighty. She had big cheekbones, dark eyes, brown skin and long white hair tied back under a kerchief like the one my grandmother wore. She was obviously Native. I put the box I was holding back on the shelf and walked over to her.

"Let me help you," I said.

She looked at me kindly. Then, as I got close, her expression changed. She looked scared. She started backing away from me quickly, with her hands up in front of her.

"No!" she said. "Get away!"

I looked behind me. I couldn't believe she was shouting at me.

"Lady," I said, "chill out. I'm just trying to help you."

"I didn't invite you," she said. "You are not welcome here!"

She backed away faster, and when she tried to turn, her feet slipped out from beneath her. I hurried toward her. She scrambled to her feet and began trotting toward the exit. I couldn't understand why she was so scared. I wanted to show her that I wasn't a threat. Plus, I didn't want any heat from security or the cops. So I followed her.

She tried to round a corner and ran straight into another old lady's shopping cart and tipped it over. Amy came out of the next aisle to see what the noise was all about. She saw me approach the old lady, who was scrambling amid the cans and boxes and trying to get to her feet.

"Ma'am," I said, "it's all right. I'm only trying to help you."

"You're not welcome here," she said again. "Go back where you came from."

Amy looked at me curiously. The manager came hotfooting over and bent to help the woman to her feet. But his feet slipped in some spilled milk, and he tumbled down beside her. Amy went to the woman and knelt beside her.

"What is it?" Amy asked. "What can I do to help you?"

The old lady clutched Amy's arm. Hard. She pointed at me.

"Him Standing," she said shakily, almost in tears. "Him Standing."

"What?" I said. "Me?"

"You are not welcome. I did not invite you," the woman said.

Amy helped her to her feet. The woman just stood there for a moment. Then she grabbed Amy by the elbows and looked into her eyes.

"The shaman has returned," she said.

"What shaman?" Amy asked.

The woman pointed a shaking finger at me.

"There," she said.

"That's my boyfriend," Amy said quietly. "That's Lucas."

"No," the old lady said. "No!"

She broke Amy's grip and again made for the exit. We looked at each other. When we tried to go after her, the manager and a security guard blocked our way.

"Sir," the security guard said, "you're going to have to come with me."

CHAPTER NINE

I explained what had happened as best I could. After checking the tapes from the security cameras and seeing that I had never touched the old woman in any way, they let me go. There was nothing they could hold me for. Amy was waiting outside the security office. When she saw me, she ran up and gave me a big hug.

"Lucas," she said, "what was that? Why was that woman so terrified of you?"

"I don't know," I said. "What was it she called me?"

"It was odd. A name, I think."

"Him Standing," I said. *"The shaman has returned."*

"Yes. That's what she said."

"What does it mean?"

"I have no idea. It was weird though. Really, really weird."

"Got that right."

We walked past the mess in the aisle. The janitor was sweeping up the dry goods. His partner had a mop and was sopping up the spills. I shook my head at the weirdness of it all. Amy grabbed my arm and stopped me in my tracks.

"Lucas," she said, "what's that?"

She pointed to something lying just under the edge of the shelving. It looked to be a small feather. I got on my hands and knees and slid it out. I picked it up and handed it to Amy. It was a small brown feather with speckled bits of brown and white at its bottom end. The spine was decorated with three tiny beads and a loop of leather thong. The beads were wonderful.

"What are they?" I asked.

Amy studied them awhile and rubbed them with the nub of a finger.

"Glass," she said. "They look handmade."

"People make handmade glass?"

"Artists do. They use a torch to melt glass together to make beads."

"What do you mean?".

"Look at the beads. Do you see how they have all kinds of different swirls of color in them?"

"Yeah. So?"

"So," she said with a smile, "a glass artist heats glass into a blob with a metal rod through the middle. Then they turn it so it gets round. Then they melt other colors of glass into the original blob and create unique kinds of beads. That's what this is."

"You know a lot about this," I said, impressed.

"I have a lot of jewelry that's made out of glass. I read up about how they make it."

"So you think the old lady made this?"

"Yeah," she said. "Maybe. Or she bought it from someone who works with feathers and Indian kinds of materials."

"It's nice," I said. "We should get it back to her."

"And maybe we could ask her what she meant by all that shaman stuff," Amy said. "I don't know what she meant by *you are not invited* either. It was weird."

We rode our bikes over to Amy's place. She lived in a nice condo in a cool, light pink building. The color reminded me of a drink they serve with tiny umbrellas sticking out of it. It was a nice place. I liked going there. Her place had floor-to ceiling windows that let in a lot of light, and it just felt good in there. Amy also had a lot of nice furniture and a kick-ass stereo system. She got me to listen to music I'd never heard before. I liked doing that.

She knew I was embarrassed because I was poor, but she always took care to make me feel comfortable. I never felt out of place there. But I still preferred to sleep in my room.

She had a computer too. After we'd eaten and had some coffee, we went into her den to search online for places where glass beads were made and sold. It was odd, but with all the light in Amy's place, I didn't feel any of the strange things I'd felt working on the mask. She was a whiz on the computer, and it didn't take her long.

"Look, Lucas," she said, holding a finger to the screen.

I leaned in and read.

"Sally Whitebird. Fused glass from a Native perspective."

"She would know where this came from," Amy said. "And it's only a short walk away. Wanna check it out?"

"Sure," I said. "It'd be good to get a handle on this weirdness."

Amy smiled. "Nice to have you back," she said.

I kissed her. I felt safe. I felt like myself. Amy was good medicine.

We walked out of her building and headed into the neighborhood where Sally Whitebird's glass studio was. Whitebird. It sounded like an Ojibway name, but I had never met anyone called that. I wondered if she knew anything about some shaman called Him Standing, and why someone might confuse me with him. I wondered if she knew why the woman in the market would be so scared.

We found the place easily. It was small, like a cottage. There were a lot of trees and bushes in the yard, and flowers and ferns everywhere too. It looked peaceful.

Amy rang the bell and we waited. We could hear a drum and chanting. The sounds stopped, and there was a moment of silence before we heard footsteps. I took the beaded feather out of my jacket pocket and held it in front of my chest. We heard the rattle of several dead bolts, and the door opened a crack. We saw a brown eye. Then we heard a groan. Then a cry. Then the sound of a body falling to the floor.

I tried to push the door open, but the body was blocking it. I pushed harder and got it open just enough for Amy to slide between the jamb and the door. I heard her rustling around. Then the door opened and there she stood, with the body of a woman lying on the floor behind her.

"My god," she said. "It's the woman from the market, Lucas. *She's* Sally Whitebird."

CHAPTER TEN

She must have given herself a good conk on the noggin, because she didn't move at all when I moved her to her couch. She was tiny. She felt like air in my hands. Amy arranged pillows behind her head. I found the kitchen and returned with a glass of water and a cold cloth. The old lady still hadn't stirred.

Her home was what some people would call exotic. All the furniture was made of wood. There was no glass or chrome anywhere, except for mirrors. The carpets were the old-fashioned rag kind. The kind old ladies like my grandmother used to make. The only flowers were dried, and there were tree branches in the corners of the room. The branches were hung with feathers and beads like the ones we'd found. There were a couple of stuffed birds and a hornet's nest on a shelf. On the wall above a small fireplace was a bear hide. A large seashell decorated a coffee table that looked like a section of tree trunk.

"Interesting," I said.

Amy looked up from mopping the woman's brow with the cloth and scanned the room.

"She really likes to keep nature close," she said.

"Wonder what the rest of the joint looks like?" I said.

"Probably a lot like this room," Amy said. "She seems like a very rustic person."

The woman groaned. Amy laid the cloth on her forehead and took her hand. I saw the old woman squeeze it. I could see the blue of her veins through her light-brown skin. Her skin was papery and brittle-looking. Slowly she came back to herself. Her eyes fluttered and then opened, and she looked at Amy.

"You found me," she said.

"Yes," Amy said. "It wasn't hard. The Internet and all."

"A whole other kind of magic," she said, and then she looked over at me. She didn't panic. Instead, she gazed at me steadily. "I'm Sally Whitebird."

"Amy One Sky. And this is Lucas Smoke. He's my boyfriend, like I told you at the market."

"He did not follow you here," she said.

"Who?" I asked.

"Him Standing," she said. "Or his agent." Amy held the water glass to Sally Whitebird's mouth, and she took a small sip. Then she lay back against the pillows and closed her eyes. Amy looked at me with a worried expression.

I whirled one finger around my ear, and she frowned at me.

"You were really scared at the market," Amy said. "You thought Lucas was someone else."

Sally groaned and put her forearm over her eyes. She breathed deeply and steadily for a few moments.

"He was there. I saw him in your face." She turned to me and looked at me with clear, dark eyes. "His shadow was all around you."

"But he's not here right now?" I asked.

"No. You've been to a place of light."

"What does that mean?" Amy asked.

"The dark shamans do not like light. It robs them of their energy."

"We were at Amy's," I said.

"A place of light?" she asked and blinked.

"Yeah," I said. "It always has been for me. I like it there: Different from where I live."

"He cannot venture there. It is a strong place. Like here. Dark medicine cannot enter here. There is too much shining, good energy."

"That's why you're not afraid of me now?" I asked.

"Yes," she replied. "I was scared at the door. But not now. Now I see that things have come to their proper place."

"We don't understand any of this," Amy said. "Our lives have actually been really strange this last little while."

"He is trying to return," Sally said. "He has been gone for generations, and I once thought that no one knew of him anymore, that he existed only as a legend."

"Bring a legend to life," I said.

"What?" Sally asked. She struggled to sit upright, and Amy reached out to help her. She was so small, her feet barely reached the floor.

I told her about Gareth Knight. I told her about his challenge on the boardwalk and about the big lump of money he gave me.

She listened intently. So I told her about my grandfather, and how he'd passed his carving skills on to me. I told her about the trick with the knife that I could do. Then I told her about Knight's directions for me to dream and carve a spirit mask to bring a legend back to life.

"Only I never saw a legend. I only ever saw the face. A painted face."

"Black. With three wavy red lines down one side. The right side," Sally whispered.

"Yes. Does that mean something?"

"It is not the heart side," Sally said. "It means he does not feel like we do. His emotions are blocked. He is a weaver of dark magic."

"And Gareth Knight?" Amy asked. "How does he fit into this?"

"A man dressed in black is the agent of the dark shaman. He is a summoner, a follower of Him Standing's medicine way. He is a shaman himself but without the great power of Him Standing. He wants the spirit of the dark shaman to inhabit the mask so he can wear it and assume that power."

"How did he find his way to me?" I asked.

Sally crossed the room and picked up a rattle made from a turtle shell. She shook it in a wide circle. It sounded old and powerful.

"Your grandfather knew these things. He put legends into spirit masks. When he taught you, that energy was transferred to you."

"But he never told me anything about any of this. He only taught me to carve," I said.

"That is the weakness they take advantage of," Sally said and shook the rattle again. "Those who know the how of things but not the why. They know how to do things but not the spiritual reason they do them."

"What do we do then?" I asked.

She looked at me with iron eyes.

"We fight," she said.

CHAPTER ELEVEN

The way Sally told the story, it seemed like a movie she'd seen. Him Standing was a member of a dark-medicine society. They were wizards. Sorcerers. They were at war with the shamans of light. The good-medicine people. The dark shamans wanted to control people, make them do their bidding. To make themselves more powerful. The shamans of light worked with the people to make them stronger. To guide them in spiritual ways that would keep them safe and strong. They were a threat to the wizards. As long as they were around to make people stronger, the dark medicine had less power. So the dark shamans created powerful magic that robbed people of their power. They were scary. They were heartless. They were the reason behind wars. Their power was in the fear they created.

Him Standing was the most powerful of the dark shamans. He had been raised with good-medicine people. But a dark master offered him riches and power. He was only a boy and was easily swayed. He became the dark master's student, and he learned quickly. By the time he was a young man, Him Standing was feared far and wide. Sally said it was because he understood both kinds of medicine and combined them to build his power. All he had to do was stand at the edge of a village, and the people fell under his control. A lot of good-medicine people died fighting him.

But a wise shaman named Otter Tail found a way to beat him. One winter he challenged Him Standing to a race. They would race across a frozen lake. The first to make it across and back would win the right to work with the people of the village, who stood on the shore to watch. Him Standing laughed. The good shaman was small. There was no way he could match the wizard's strength and speed.

At first, Him Standing was far ahead. Otter Tail only walked. When he got to the far side, the dark shaman roared with laughter. It echoed off the hills. The people were scared. He began to run in big thumping bounds back across the lake. He followed his own tracks through the snow.

But he was heavy. The first crossing had weakened the ice. The second time he crossed the lake, the ice broke. Him Standing fell into the freezing water. His anger was huge.

His strength was enormous. He swung at the edge of the ice to try to get a grip. But his anger only broke more of it off.

He tried to use his magic to call fish to swim under him and lift him up. But the cold weakened him. No fish came to his rescue. He was drowning.

Otter Tail stood yards away from the hole in the ice.

"You must help me!" Him Standing said.

"Why?" Otter Tail asked.

"Because you are good," Him Standing gasped.

"You were good once."

"I know. I am sorry. I will change."

"How do I know this is true?" Otter Tail asked.

"I give my word," Him Standing said. "Please."

"Let us make a trade then," Otter Tail said.

"Yes. Anything."

"I will trade you worlds. I will spare you, but you must reside forever in the dream world."

"If I do not agree?" Him Standing asked. His teeth were chattering. His grip on the ice was loosening.

"Then die and have no world," Otter Tail said.

Him Standing bobbed under. He flailed in the water. He got a grip on the edge of the ice again. His head was barely above the surface.

"Yes. All right. I will take your deal."

With that, Otter Tail took a turtle-shell rattle from his robes. He shook it in a wide circle around Him Standing. He spoke in words they didn't understand. The people on the shore watched in amazement as the wizard was lifted from the water. He spun rapidly in the air. Then he vanished.

Sally paused and looked at me steadily. "He went to the dream world. He has lived there ever since. His followers have tried to bring him back many times. But they needed a source of pure magic."

"Me?" I asked.

"Yes," Sally said. "Your grandfather shared his gift with you. But you had it in you already. That is why you create so easily. That is why you do what you do without study. It is pure magic."

"Gareth Knight saw that on the board-walk that day," Amy said.

"Yes. He recognized it. Lucas is Ojibway. So was Him Standing. It must have seemed too good to be true for him," Sally said.

"Knight is a dark shaman?" I asked.

"Yes. But not one with true power. Not yet. He needs the mask."

"What about the mask?" Amy asked. "Why did Lucas carve his own face and not Him Standing's?"

"Him Standing lives in the dream world. Otter Tail did not tell him that the dream world and our world exist in the same time and place but do not meet. There is no doorway," Sally said.

"But that's what he said. *The doorway is open*," Amy said. "I heard Lucas say that."

"Lucas has changed, hasn't he?" Sally asked.

"Yes," Amy said. "It scares me."

"He goes to the dream world. There he is under the power of Him Standing. The dark shaman becomes real through Lucas. The more he dreams, the more he carves. More dark magic goes into the mask."

"I am the doorway," I said. "When it's finished, it will hold the spirit of Him Standing."

"And all of his power," Amy whispered.

"Yes," Sally said. "He is coming through you and into the mask."

"A spirit mask," I said quietly.

"There are good and bad spirits," Sally said. "Your grandfather did not teach you this. It is the weakness they looked for."

"This is really freaking me out," I said. "How are we supposed to fight something like this?"

Sally reached over and took my hand. "Finish the mask," she said.

"What if I can't?"

"What do you think might prevent you from finishing?"

"Fear," I said quietly.

"Fear is a magic of its own, Lucas."

"What do you mean?"

She smiled. "Fear is a power that we all have. Except we are never taught to accept it as a power. We get taught that it is a weakness. We are ashamed of it. We think it makes us less. But in fact it makes us more.

"It's only when we walk fully into it that fear shows its powerful side. The darkness isn't the absence of light. It's the threshold of light. When you are courageous enough to stand in your fear, you are learning how to step forward into the light."

I looked at the floor and considered what she'd said. "Are you telling me that if I finish the mask, even though it terrifies me to think about it, everything will be okay?

"No," she said. "I'm telling you that you will be okay. That's what is certain."

"I still don't understand."

She took my hands in hers. "Walking through your fear makes you stronger. It makes you able to walk through other fears. It gives you courage. It gives you faith that there are bigger powers in the world than fear. When you walk through fear, you, Lucas, become a bigger power than the fear. It is its own medicine in the end."

"What do you mean?"

"The only way to conquer fear is by facing it."

I looked at her. She was calm. She was still and placid, and her hands were warm. She gave me a little smile, and I felt it in my chest. I trusted her. "I'll finish the mask," I said.

CHAPTER TWELVE

I spent that night at Amy's for the first time. It felt good. We cooked supper. Then we sat on her balcony and watched the sun go down. After that we sat in candlelight and listened to music. Then we went to bed. We snuggled. We held each other. We fell asleep in each other's arms. For the first time since all of this started I didn't dream.

Amy had a photo shoot in the morning, so we got up early and went our separate ways. I took a long, leisurely ride through the city.

The story Sally had told us made me jittery. But the ride through the city calmed me.

When I got to the rooming house, Gareth Knight was waiting in my room. I knew he would be there, but I faked surprise.

He was dressed like a punk. He had on black sneakers. He wore tight black jeans and a torn-up old black T-shirt. There was a black kerchief at his throat. He wore black eye makeup and black lipstick. His hair was spiked with gel. His arms were covered in tattoos made with black ink. They were of symbols I'd never seen before. He was sitting at my work table, drumming his fingers.

"Where have you been?" he asked, tilting his head and arching one eyebrow.

"Had to get out," I said. "Been working hard."

"Yes. But I need results, Lucas. Vacation on your own time. Now, where were you?"

"I told you I just needed to get away, that's all. I didn't go anywhere special."

"Ah. Ms. One Sky's, I take it. Where does the dear girl live, anyway?"

Sally had told me that he would want to know. "She has a place by the river," I said.

"It's a long river, Lucas."

"Well, she's becoming a famous model. She doesn't want just anyone knowing where she lives."

Knight smiled and rubbed at the tattoo on his forearm. "Don't get cute with me, Lucas."

Sally had told me that dark shamans existed on pride. They would never ask a question twice. It would mean they were weak. It would mean they didn't have power over someone. So I took a risk in order to protect Amy. "Hey, I'm not being cute. I'm just saying that you don't need to know where my girl lives. That's all."

"Ah, rebellion. I so love that energy. It feels so good to control." Knight stood up and stared at me. He raised a hand. I felt invisible fingers at my throat. Then I was lifted off the floor. I hung suspended three feet in the air. Choking.

Sally had told me too that anger was a dark shaman's weakness. If I could get him to express it, to reveal himself, he would have less of a hold. The grip he had was strong. I was scared. But knowledge is a weapon, and I held on to Sally's teaching. I waved a hand weakly in surrender. I was lowered to the floor.

I gasped and bent over to catch my breath. I could feel Knight waiting. I fought to get my breathing back. But I was happy to see him lose control. The other thing Sally had said was that it was important to get him to declare himself. If a wizard admitted who he was, he lost even more power.

"Neat trick," I said hoarsely. "Where'd you learn that, at some cheap magic school?"

"Cheap magic?" Knight asked. He sat back down on the chair and folded one leg over the other. "What I possess is not some party magician's bag of tricks. I'm not a buffoon, Lucas."

"What are you then?" I asked. "I know you're not just some moneyed-up art lover."

He smiled and scratched at his chin. He studied me intently. He nodded his head slowly.

"I'm a member of a very special club," he said. "Elite, really. There aren't a lot of us around."

"Big deal," I said. My voice was coming back. "I could say the same about me. There aren't a lot of guys like me around either. That's why you want me. I'm—what did you say? Elite?"

He laughed. "You're common. A dime a dozen. I could find someone like you on any street corner or any boardwalk. In fact, I did."

"Yeah? So where do elite dudes like you hang out?"

"Hang out? We don't hang out, Lucas. We exist."

"So where do you exist then?"

Knight stood up. I could tell he was irritated. He shrugged his shoulders and shook his head and then spread his arms wide. He shook his hands. The room started to shake. My dishes rattled on the shelf. A few books tumbled. The air got hot, and it was hard to breathe. He rose slowly off the floor and spun lazily in a circle. Then he floated to the floor again. The room returned to normal.

He took a quick step toward me, and I shrank back against the wall. He smiled. He leaned in close to me. I could feel his hot breath on my face. His eyes locked with mine. They were dark and glittering.

"We exist on your fear, boy. We exist in your dark corners."

I grinned. I could see the rage in his eyes.

"Kinda vague for the elite. Don't you think?" I said.

Knight fumed.

"I am a shaman, if you must know. I am a grand wizard."

"So grand you gotta get a common person like me to do your work for you? Carve your own mask then, Merlin."

I felt the invisible grip on my throat again. I was lifted off the floor again. He shook me, and I thought he was really going to lose it. I could see how far gone with anger he was. He fought to regain his calm, and I slid back to the floor.

"Finish the mask," he said firmly. "Or feel the force of my magic."

Then he turned and was gone.

CHAPTER THIRTEEN

"So you were able to get him to rise to anger?" Sally asked.

"More than that," I said. "The guy lost it."

"That's good. He needs the mask more than I thought. He needs it to give him a way to grab more power."

"He didn't seem to be short of any juice," I said, rubbing my throat.

"There is far more power to be gained than what he already has," Sally said.

"I can hardly wait," I said with a wince.

"What do we do now?" Amy asked.

We were sitting in Sally's backyard. She'd made a strong black tea that she said would give me the mental strength I needed to handle what was coming. That didn't sound so great to me, but I drank it anyway. It tasted awful. But something about the old lady told me I could trust her with everything. I did. Amy did too. We both drank our fair share of that rough tea.

"The good thing is that Knight has not been this way before. He has never found anyone with the gift your grandfather gave to you, Lucas. It means that even he does not know exactly what to expect. That's what our advantage is," Sally said. "We need to convince him that the spell and the hold of the dreams are working."

"They are," Amy said. "You told us that much yourself."

"Yes, but as long as Lucas comes to places of light, he is safe. The hold is broken for a short time, and that weakens it."

"So what are you saying?" I asked.

"I'm saying you need to be very careful. If Knight gets any idea that you have found a measure of safety, of light, you will be in great danger."

"Oh good," I said. "I thought you meant I had something to worry about."

Amy took my hand and squeezed it. Sally regarded both of us with concern.

"He may use the power he has now to imprison you, or worse. Dark shamans are soul stealers. You risk everything if you continue."

"Why don't I just disappear then? Take off. Split. Boogie."

"You can't," she said. "You know the truth. You know that the power of Him Standing can be brought into this world. If it is not through you, Knight will find someone else."

"Because I'm common. A dime a dozen, like he said."

Sally took both of my hands in hers and cradled them. She looked at the ground for a while. When she looked back up at me, she was crying.

"You are not common, Lucas. You are special. That's why Knight values you. You carry a gift. You are able to see the essence of things, their spirit. That kind of vision is not an everyday kind. But there are others. Knight will be drawn to their energy just as he was drawn to yours. Their fate will be the same."

"What fate is that?" Amy asked quietly.

There was a long beat of silence. We could hear traffic on the street, the birds in the trees, the wind. Sally raised her face and looked up at the sky.

"This world and the dream world are full," she said. "What is taken from one must be replaced by something of the other. There must always be a balance."

"Are you saying what I think you're saying?" I asked.

"Yes," she said quietly. "When the spirit of Him Standing enters this world, your spirit, or whoever Knight finds to do the work, will take his place. It will be imprisoned in the dream world forever."

"Oh my god," Amy said. "In limbo."

Sally could only shake her head.

* * *

That night I had a powerful dream. It started normal enough. But then it changed into something so sharp and real, I could still taste and feel everything about it when I woke up. I was walking across a wide prairie. The wind was blowing, and the sky was filled with clouds. They flew like giant sailing ships across the ocean of the sky. There were a few thousand buffalo grazing in the distance. I could smell them.

It was getting close to sunset. The western sky was on fire with so many colors, it was blinding. There was a fire in a small canyon. I could smell meat roasting. I could hear the wood crackling. I was suddenly very hungry, and I walked toward the fire. There was a man there wrapped in a blanket and poking at the fire with a stick.

As I got nearer, he turned to face me. I stopped dead in my tracks. Nothing moved in the dream then. There were no sounds and no smells. There was only the face of the man at the fire. My grandfather.

"Come sit, Grandson," he said. "I have been waiting for you. This buffalo roast is nearly ready."

I felt as though I floated to the fire. I couldn't feel my feet moving. When I got there, he waved me to a seat across from him and handed me a wooden cup filled with tea. It was Sally's tea. He smiled at me.

"How can you be here?" I asked.

"It is the dream world, Grandson. All things are possible here."

"My dreams have been scary."

"I know. But there are two sides, just as there are in your world."

"Light and dark," I said.

He nodded.

"In all things there must be balance. There are always two sides. Two faces." He looked at me solemnly as he spoke, and I realized for the first time in a long time how much I missed him.

He turned to the fire to tend to the meat. When he looked at me again, he was a young man. Then I watched as his face aged back to the one I remembered.

"Two faces, Grandson," he said. "To everything."

When I woke up, I knew exactly what I had to do.

CHAPTER FOURTEEN

The next time Knight saw me, I was in horrible shape. I hadn't eaten. Hadn't washed. I was still wearing the same clothes he'd last seen me in. The bones jutted out from under my skin, which was yellow and sickly-looking. My eyes were red. They bulged like a madman's in a very haggard, worn face. I could hear the rattle of my breath in my chest. In spite of this, he smiled when he saw me.

"The work goes well, I see," he said. He was dressed in a black tuxedo with a black shirt. His shoes gleamed with a glossy sheen. His black cane rested on his thigh when he sat down to look at me.

"May I see it?"

"No!" I shouted and stood up quickly. I waved a fist in the air. "No one can lay eyes on this before it is finished. No one can see the doorway but me."

"My, my. You have been getting on, haven't you?" Knight said.

"I dream all the time," I said. "The vision gets clearer and clearer, and I can't stop working."

"Good. Good," he said. "You're under the spell of it."

"Yeah," I said and slumped back into my chair facing the work table. "He's so strong, so powerful. His face is incredible."

"He was a leader like no other. He was a magician. He could do things never seen before or since."

"A black shaman," I mumbled.

"That's what the fearful called him. What they call those of us who follow his teachings."

"He admires you," I said. I was staring at the cloth that covered the mask. I didn't blink. I stared and didn't move. I could feel him watching me.

"Does he now? And why would that be, Lucas?"

"No one has ever tried to call him forward before. No one has ever thought it was possible. No one was ever a grand wizard like you."

"Well, I am truly honored to be held in such esteem," he said.

I turned to look at him. My face poured sweat, and I wiped at my eyes with a sleeve. I sat back in my chair with my legs spread wide. My hands dangled between my knees. My mouth hung open and my eyelids were half closed.

"He wants to live in you," I mumbled. A thin line of drool leaked from my lips.

"In me? I expected his power to reside in the mask."

There was a sudden chill in the room. It crept out from the walls, and we could see our breath. The lights flickered. They grew dim. The shadows in the corners seemed to move toward us. I could see Knight growing anxious. When I spoke again, the voice that came out of me was hollow. I didn't recognize it, even though I could feel my lips moving. "The boy was a poor choice. He is weak. He has no knowledge. There is no power in him."

"Master?" Knight asked. He leaned in to peer at my face.

"Whom else did you expect? The boy's hands have opened the doorway. It is as you wished to be."

"When, Master? When will you step through?"

"He inscribes a spell within the wood. The spell is the source of my power. It is the source of your own. The mask will contain it. Whoever wears the mask owns the power. When it is finished, I will come."

"Does he know? Does he have any clue to what we do?" Knight asked.

"Look at him. Does he look like one who has any wisdom?"

Knight studied me. He stared for a long moment, then waved a hand slowly in front of my eyes. I did not blink. I was locked in a trance. The only motion from my body was a twitching and another slide of drool from my mouth.

"He is not here," Knight said.

"He will not be. His dreams are my dreams. I send them to him. Even when he is awake, I send them. He lives in them now. This is how I give him the words to the spell he carves into the wood. He does not know anything."

"You're sure?"

There was a sudden roaring in the room. It was like the howl of an animal. But it was also like the screams of a horde of people in agony. It flew around the room in a circle. It echoed off every wall. It gained speed and volume. It became a tornado. Cupboard doors flew open. The closet door smashed against the wall, and the windows rattled in their frames. The lights went out, then flickered back to life. The room was a mess. The roaring died down.

Knight's face showed amazement. He looked at me where I dangled in the air, my arms hanging limply at my side. Then I spun in a slow, lazy circle, just as he had done. It seemed to take forever. Finally I was set down in my chair, and my head slumped forward onto my chest. Then my head snapped up again, and I stared hard at Knight. He cringed a little in his seat.

"You dare to question me?" The voice that came from me was savage.

Time seemed to stop.

"Who you are is because of me. What you know is what I have taught. Your power is my power. Do I need to convince you of this? Do you doubt who has power here?" The voice was huge and thundered in the room.

"No, Master," Knight said quietly. "I do not doubt you."

"Then leave me be. Let the boy finish what he has begun. I will summon you when the time is right."

"Yes, Master," Knight said and stood up.

He looked at me. I was slumped back in the chair. I heard him close the door, and then everything was silent. It was a long time before I could get back to the carving again.

CHAPTER FIFTEEN

I'd never learned to speak Ojibway. By the time I was born, our lives had changed. The old ways were dying out. Most of the people around me when I was a kid spoke English. Anytime I heard someone say something in our language, it always sounded weird to me. Even on the playground and in the games we played as kids, we always yelled at each other in English. So I never got used to it. It was always something I kinda meant to learn when I had the time. I just never found that time.

So carving words into the inside of the mask was hard. But it was hard for two other reasons, as well. The first was that they came while I was in dream time. The second was that there were a lot of them. It took a lot to carve them into the wood. And they weren't what I'd call words at all. They were symbols. They were these little scratchings and hen pecks that looked like things a kid would do.

I lost time. I disappeared. I bent to the wood with my chisel and knives, and the night would vanish. I don't know where I went. All I knew was that when I came out of it, I was tired. I could barely sit up in my chair. Now when I collapsed into my bed and slept, I slept without dreams. I just sank into it.

Most times it was noon or later when I came to. Once I got my feet under me, I made my way to Amy's. The place of light. The first time she saw me, she was shocked.

"My god, Lucas," she gasped. "What's happening to you?"

"I'm finishing the mask," I said.

"But your face. And your body. It looks as though it's eating you up."

"Feels like it too," I said. "What have you been doing?"

"Sally's been teaching me," she said.

"Teaching you what?"

"Stuff about our ceremonies. Things I never knew about how our people understood the universe."

"Secret stuff?" I asked.

She studied me for a long moment.

"No," she said finally. "Only stuff that we forget to ask about. I know that, living in the city, I forget about stuff like that."

"Me too," I said. "This whole thing's like a big giant puzzle to me, and I feel like somebody stole some of the most important pieces."

"Me too. It scares me, but it thrills me at the same time."

"How?" I asked.

"Well, it's kinda like you said—someone stole some of the important pieces. I feel like this is showing me what parts of my own puzzle I've been missing."

I looked out the window to think over what she had said. I felt better. I felt real. I felt safe, like the old lady had said I would. I let that feeling wash over me and fill me. When I looked at her again, I smiled.

"I never knew how incomplete I felt," I said and took her hand. "I dreamt of my grandfather. We sat together just like in the old days. I think he meant to give me those pieces, but he was gone before he had the chance. After that, nothing really seemed to matter anymore, and I left it all and came here. Now I know how much I walked away from."

"Does it make you sad?" she asked quietly.

"Yeah, "I said. "Angry too."

"At yourself?"

"Not so much, but some at me for wasting it."

"You're not wasting it. You're carrying on your grandfather's gift. You're bringing it to a whole new group of people."

"I guess," I said. "But is that enough, you think? Does working without a foundation matter in the end?"

"It does if you bring your heart to it," Amy said. "You do that. It's what makes you great."

She smiled. I stood up and walked to her and gave her a hug. We held on to each other for a good long time without speaking.

"There's a secret I need to tell you," I whispered in her ear.

"Does Sally know?" she asked.

"Yes," I said. "She does."

CHAPTER SIXTEEN

Sally found a spot for me to give the mask to Knight. She said it needed to be a place that held good energy. It had to be a place that was peaceful. Most important, it had to be a place that he had never been before. It had to be a place of light that didn't look like one. When I told her I had finished the mask, she found the spot in less than a day.

I left a note with directions for Knight in my room. The three of us went to the spot to wait for him. It was at a bend in the river about three miles beyond the city limits.

"In the old days this was a gathering place," Sally said. She was wearing a pale buckskin dress with fringes, a plain red cloth head band and plain moccasins without beadwork. She looked like a grandmother. "The good hearts would gather here for ceremonies. When the city grew, it never seemed able to reach this place. It spread out in other directions but not in this one."

"No one knew its history?" Amy asked.

"Some could get it sometimes," Sally said. "But sacred places tell their story by feeling."

"Is that how you found this place?" I asked. "Or have you been here before?"

"It called to me," she said and smiled. "When I sent out good thoughts for a safe place for you to offer the mask, I felt this place. It was easy to find."

There were thick bushes around a clearing in the trees. The grass was about knee-high. The wind made a soft whisper as it moved through the leaves and the grass.

The river gurgled at the far edge of the clearing. We could hear birdsong and the splashes of fish jumping. It felt like we were in a place that existed beyond time.

Sally directed me to press the grass flat with my feet in a circle in the middle of the clearing. I was carrying the mask in a big canvas sack, and she told me to set it on the ground in the middle of the circle I had made.

"When he comes, make him ask for it," she said. "He has to make a request for power."

When I'd finished, Sally and Amy picked out a spot in the bushes where they could not be seen. I was left alone in the clearing to wait for Knight.

It didn't take long.

He just appeared. One minute I was alone, the next he was there. There was the hint of a smile on his face. He wore black denim and cowboy boots. His hat was a neat little black bowler.

"I must admit, Lucas, I like the back-to-nature touch," he said. "It's fitting. Very noble-savage and all that."

"Well, after all this work, I need some fresh air," I said.

He pointed to the sack at my feet.

"That's it then?"

"Yes. I think you'll like the handiwork."

"Oh, it's more than mere handiwork, Lucas. It's magic."

"Magic takes a lot of work," I said.

"Yes," he said, stroking his chin. "Sometimes it does. May I see it?"

"Excuse me," I said.

He tilted his head and grinned at me.

"How quaint. The artist struggles to let go of his creation. His baby."

"Something like that."

"Well, okay. Lucas, may I have the mask?"

"Sure," I said, smiling. "It was yours all the time. I made it for you."

I bent to retrieve the mask from the canvas sack. I caught a glimpse of Amy and Sally staring out at me from a break in the bushes. They were lying flat on the ground, watching. The fact that Knight did not know they were there gave me hope. He was not all-powerful. When I stood up, I held the mask behind my back.

"It didn't turn out the way I thought it would," I said.

"True art never does, does it?" Knight asked. He took a step closer to me, his hand outstretched.

"I suppose not," I replied. "But I never figured on carving this." I pulled the mask out from behind my back and held it out to him. It was a perfect copy of my own face, but I'd painted it black with three red wavy lines down the right side.

Knight's mouth dropped open. He took very slow steps toward me, and his hand shook a little as he neared the mask. I felt the wind stop. Everything went silent. The air grew thicker, heavier. I could hear the rustle of the grass with every step he took.

"The master," he whispered.

I put the mask in his hands. It was apparent that he had never seen the face of Him Standing and had no idea how the mask was supposed to look in the end. He stood with his head bent, and I thought I heard him sigh. He rubbed the symbols on the inside of the mask with the fingertips of one hand.

"The doorway," he said. "The words to open the doorway. When I put the mask to my face, they will be given to me."

"It's what the dreams told me," I said. "I put them there exactly as they came to me from the dream world."

"This is what my associates and I have wanted for a very long time," he said. "They will be pleased when I return with the master."

"With the mask, you mean?"

Knight raised his head and stared at me. There was a question in his eyes.

"I mean that when I put the mask to my face and open the doorway, the master will emerge," he said. "It is what is foretold."

"Maybe in your circles," I said. "In my circles, in my dreams, in my art, I was told to make this."

I went down on one knee and rustled about in the canvas sack. I looked up at Knight. He was watching intently. I slowly stood up, my back toward him. When I turned to face him, he was stunned by the second mask I wore on my face.

CHAPTER SEVENTEEN

There was a sudden roll of thunder. The sky was clear, but I heard the thunder clearly. Knight glared at me. Behind him, the trees and bushes were swaying. But there was no wind. I smelled something foul in the air.

"You dare to play games with me, Lucas? I have the mask that opens the doorway," Knight said. He took a few steps toward me, the mask held up to his face. "In a few moments, none of this will matter at all."

I rubbed the face of the mask I was wearing. It was a man's face. It was an old face. It was a face built of angles and juts and shadows. It was a face with eyes that squinted behind deep creases and lines. It was the face of a man who had known things—secrets, spells, charms, songs and prayers. It was the face of a shaman.

"You're not the only one with a mask of power, Knight," I said.

"Really?" he sneered. "Do you think you have what it takes to go against me? You know nothing."

"I know that you don't have enough juice to get Him Standing through the doorway on your own. If you did, you wouldn't have needed me."

"I told you. People like you are a dime a dozen. I would have found someone else who knows how to do a trick with a knife." He eased the mask to the side and smiled at me.

"Maybe," I said. "But no one who could have gotten the symbols you need. I did that."

"The symbols, yes. I confess that surprised me. But what surprised me more is the voice that came from you that day. It was clearly the master's voice."

Sally stepped out from behind the bushes. Her hands were behind her back, and she stood straight while the same energy that made the trees sway whipped her hair around.

"He's never heard the voice, Lucas," she said.

Knight spun around quickly. "Who is this? Another one of your little secrets, Lucas?"

Sally sidestepped carefully around him. Knight turned slowly, following her with his eyes. When Sally stood next to me, she took what she held behind her back and handed it to me. When Knight saw the large turtle-shell rattle, he screamed with anger. A sudden crash of lightning from the sky turned everything blue-white. When I took the rattle and turned to Knight, he was floating inches off the ground.

"I don't know who you are," he said to Sally. "But you are small and weak like him. Nothing you bring has the power to stop what I have put into motion."

Sally looked at him squarely. She didn't waver. She gazed at Knight, and I was proud of her courage.

"Raise the rattle," I heard her say.

I lifted the rattle up above my head. I felt my feet leave the ground. Knight and I now both hovered above the clearing in the trees. He laughed. Then he spun in a slow circle. It was my turn to laugh.

"I've seen that before, Gareth. It doesn't rattle me." I grinned at the bad pun.

"Maybe this will then," he said. He held both hands out toward me. Lightning bolts shrieked toward me.

I held the rattle out, and both bolts bounced off it and into the sky. Then I felt the taut strength of invisible hands at my throat. They squeezed. They were crushing. I began to feel the dark edge of unconsciousness. But there was something else. There was the face of the man I'd carved into the mask. He emerged from the darkness. His face hung suspended against nothingness.

"Move the rattle in a circle," he said calmly. "Shake it lightly in as wide a circle as you can."

My hands were weak, but I did as he said. As I made the circle in the air, I smelled the burn of lightning, and my feet touched down on the ground again. The grip on my throat was gone.

"Speak the words," the shaman said.

I began to say the words behind the symbols carved into the mask Knight wore. It was hard. I had never spoken the language. But I had heard them in the dreams while I carved the symbols, and I remembered the sound of them. I spoke slowly at first, unsure of myself, and Knight simply stared, his eyes wide with shock.

When I started to speak with more confidence, his expression turned to panic.

"What are you doing? How did you learn this spell?" he yelled. There was a sudden wind whipping around him.

"Dreams," I said, breaking off from the stream of words. I shook the rattle at him. "They are Otter Tail's words, and this is Otter Tail's face I wear."

"No!" he screamed.

He began tugging at the edge of his mask, but it wouldn't budge. He ran about in a circle, pulling at the mask with both hands. He collapsed onto the ground. He rolled about frantically. There was a cloud of dust around him as he wrestled with the painted mask latched to his face. He was screaming in fear.

I shook the rattle in a circle and kept on reciting the words. The wind spun into a tight circle. Knight was lifted off the ground.

Amy and Sally walked slowly toward me. We all watched Knight continue to struggle to get the mask off his face. They stood behind me as I continued speaking the ancient words. The wind grew wilder. Yet it blew only around him. Where we stood, it was calm and cool.

Finally he tired. He hung in the air, limp and wasted.

"How?" he croaked. "How is this possible?"

"You said it yourself, Gareth," I said. "I have the gift to open the doorway."

"But I wear the mask," he sputtered.

"You wear *a* mask. There are two faces to everything," I said. "All things must be in balance. This mask that I wear is the opposite of yours. When something comes out of the dream world, something must go back into it."

"No!"

"Yes. Your wish was to be one with your master. Well, now you can be." I shook the rattle in a wider, faster circle, and he spun in the air. I shook it faster and he spun faster. When his spinning matched the speed of the wind around him, he vanished like Him Standing had vanished long ago.

The wind died down. I collapsed. I could barely breathe.

I felt Sally removing the mask from my face. The air revived me. I opened my eyes, and Amy was kneeling at my side.

"Lucas," she said, "why didn't you tell me about Otter Tail when you told me your grandfather taught you how to fight this?"

"I couldn't risk Knight getting to you. I told you as much as I could and still keep you safe."

"You spoke the language."

"He gave it to me in the dreams."

"Him Standing never knew what you were doing?"

"It wasn't his dream," I said. "No one owns the dream world, Amy. No one owns dreams. They're for everybody. That's another thing my grandfather gave me."

"So Otter Tail was there all the time?"

"Yes."

"Waiting for you?"

"For someone," I said. "Knight said it best. I'm not the only one who knows how to do a trick with a knife."

CHAPTER EIGHTEEN

After Knight went to the dream world, my life settled down. I finally moved in with Amy, and I found an agent to help sell my work. I didn't need people as models anymore. I had dreams. But they were different now. They were filled with light. I was able to carve amazing things that shone like legends, and the wood seemed to take on a life of its own. My work was stunning and sold well. I had the money I used to dream about.

"You know, it's funny," I said to Amy one day.

"What's funny?" she asked.

"Well, all the stuff a guy dreams about—money, cars, big shiny things?"

"Yeah?"

"They feel better as dreams."

"What do you mean?"

I laughed.

"I guess I mean that now that I have some of that dream stuff, it doesn't matter as much as the other stuff I've found."

"What kind of other stuff?"

"All I have to do is look around me. I live in a great place all filled with light with a beautiful woman who loves me. I have a great career doing something I'm good at and that I love doing. I have friends. I have enough to eat. I can come and go as I please. And I still have dreams."

She smiled and took my hand.

"And these dreams you have now? What are they about?"

"Everything," I said. "Everything I ever imagined and everything I never imagined. It's what I carve now. What I imagine."

"The stuff of dreams," she said.

Now and then, my grandfather came to visit when I dreamed. We'd sit somewhere where the wind blew warm, and he would talk to me. He'd tell me all the things that he never got around to telling me when he was with me. He filled me up with legends and stories and teachings. When I awoke from those dreams, I felt very quiet inside. I felt humble. I never dreamed of darkness again.

I still took my tools and went to the boardwalk. I still hung out there a lot. But I found kids who wanted to learn how to carve, and I taught them for free. We sat in the sun with tourists standing around us, and I showed them how to bring wood to life. I gave them the gift my grandfather gave to me.

And sometimes, when those afternoons were over, I would go and stand at the end of the boardwalk and look out over the lake. I would stare at that point where water disappears into sky. I would marvel at how they flowed into each other. I would wonder how we sometimes miss seeing such a magical thing. Sometimes when I did that, I would see my grandfather's face or Otter Tail's in that space where everything came together. I knew that I could never ever be alone again.

Sally gave me the turtle-shell rattle. I gave her the mask. What she did with it we never knew, but she told us it was in a safe and honorable place. We trusted her. She became a good friend.

"You're a shaman, aren't you?" I asked her a month or so after Knight had gone to the dream world.

"Some people use that word," she said. "But it's not one we use to refer to ourselves."

"There are more of you?" Amy asked.

She smiled. "There are always people who seek to help others find their way."

"That's what a shaman does?" I asked. "What about the magic?"

"That is the magic," she said.

I believed her.

RICHARD WAGAMESE is one of Canada's foremost Native authors and journalists. In a career spanning thirty years, he has worked in newspapers, radio, television and publishing, and has won numerous awards for his work. Awarded an Honorary Doctor of Letters degree from Thompson Rivers University in 2010, he lives outside Kamloops, British Columbia, with his wife and Molly the Story Dog.